Sweet Dreams

Sweet Dreams
Copyright © 2024 by Mellanie Crouell

Published in the United States of America

Library of Congress Control Number: 2024903911
ISBN   Paperback: 979-8-89091-537-5
ISBN   eBook: 979-8-89091-538-2

All rights reserved. No part of this publication may be reproduced, stored in a retrieval system or transmitted in any way by any means, electronic, mechanical, photocopy, recording or otherwise without the prior permission of the author except as provided by USA copyright law.

The opinions expressed by the author are not necessarily those of ReadersMagnet, LLC.

ReadersMagnet, LLC
10620 Treena Street, Suite 230 | San Diego, California, 92131 USA
1.619. 354. 2643 | www.readersmagnet.com

Book design copyright © 2024 by ReadersMagnet, LLC. All rights reserved.

Cover design by Tifanny Curaza
Interior design by Daniel Lopez

Sweet Dreams

MELLANIE CROUELL

ReadersMagnet, LLC

Dedicated to Mrs. Jennifer Elson
Third Grade Class of 2006-2007
Of
Brinson Elementary School

The men and women of US Armed Forces

Contents

Chapter One 1
Chapter Two 8
Chapter Three 12
Chapter Four 15
Chapter Five 21
Chapter Six 23
Chapter Seven 27
Chapter Eight 29
Chapter Nine 32
Chapter Ten 36
Chapter Eleven 38
Chapter Twelve 42
Chapter Thirteen 45
Chapter Fourteen 46
Chapter Fifteen 48
Chapter Sixteen 51
Chapter Seventeen 52
Chapter Eighteen 56
Chapter Nineteen 58
Chapter Twenty 61

Chapter One

I will never forget that day! Mr. Tysmens found me on the street running. I could smell the ice cream. I did not know Mrs. Pattello had open the ice cream shop up the street. The sound of the motor of the freezer sounded as if God was growling at me. Mom did the best she could. I was a handful. Dad was stationed in Iraq or Tokyo, I can't remember. I know it wasn't too long after he returned to take us to Alexandria, Virginia. Dad was stationed there for four years. When I would get the anxiety that Dad was going to have to leave in the middle of the night, Dad would say, "This is a special assignment, Leyton. I am not going nowhere right now."

It was hard! I began to believe him and enjoy it. I lost contact with a few friends throughout the years. Some I am blessed to find now that I am in the military. It is different and special that I have my own family. A lot of decisions my dad made when I was a kid, I understand them now why he made each decision. I don't know how him and mom did it. I was the kid that constantly in something or doing something, and pulling at their shirt or hand to get their attention. In my head, I hear my son, but I sigh in answering him. Now, that he is fourteen, I am still wanting to know where do this energy come from? I paused. We are out to eat. We are having some father and son time. We are here at Mrs. Pattello's ice cream shop. The name has changed since her children has taken over. It is called "Pattello's Pub and Creamery". The best ice cream and burgers in the area. The waitress puts our food on the table. I had him to wait until he finished his food. This buys me some time for me telling L.J. the story of Mr. Tysmens and I. The time was over. L.J.'s food was gone so quick, I checked to see if he chewed and swallowed. I was still eating my food. L.J. waited so nicely to let me finish my food in peace. Then, I hear this.

"Dad, tell me the story," said L.J.

"Son, you have heard this story for how many times.

"Yes, but today is going to be more special because I am in the actual place where it takes place."

"Alright, L.J.," I chuckled.

"Here is the story, I could smell the sweet fragrance of my all-time favorite strawberry ice cream. How could this be? I ran down the street looking and praying. I heard a sound that made me think Jesus was growling at me. Oh! The smell was getting stronger. I must be getting closer. I didn't see Mr. Tysmens drive up beside me while I was running."

"Leyton, Leyton, Leyton!" yelled Mr. Tysmens. "Where are you running too? What are you thinking about?"

"Mr. Tysmens, I smell that sweet fragrance," I replied.

"Oh! son. I know what it is. Mrs. Connie Pattello has opened an ice cream shop."

"What is the growling sound Mr. Tysmens?" I asked.

"Leyton, it is the motor to their freezer to keep the ice cream cold. Would you like to visit the store?" asked Mr. Tysmens. "Go tell your mother where you are going."

I ran home to tell mama. I pulled open the door and ran through the house like a force of wind. I began to yell, "Mom, where are you?" I heard Mom walking so hard upstairs until it sounded like thunder.

"Leyton Arnelle Preyson, you know how to act when you come in this house. Now what do you want young man?" She yelled back at me.

"Can I go with Mr. Tysmens to the ice cream shop down the street?" I asked.

"Yes, Leyton, you may."

"Thanks, Mom."

"Leyton, you are forgetting something?"

I laid a kiss on my Mom and she chuckled very loudly.

"You are so silly, Leyton. Be careful and behave." She cautioned.

"I will Mom." I yelled as I ran out the door.

"Leyton are you ready to go?" asked Mr. Tysemens.

"Yes, sir!" I replied. Riding down the street, the aroma was getting so strong I could taste the ice cream as if it touched my tongue. I am full of excitement. Mr. Tysmens drove up to the shop. I couldn't believe how big this shop was. It had two drive-thru windows, a parking lot the size of the Grand Canyon, and the coolest sign I ever saw. The sign was a banana split. Inside the banana in big print was "Pattello's Heavenly".

"Leyton, are you going to get out of the truck?" asked Mr. Tysmens.

I'm in amazement at how huge it is. We walk up to the shop and I open the door. The smell of strawberry ice cream hit me like a brick wall. I look around the shop, to see a long freezer with at least twenty different ice creams, and knew exactly what I want. I hear this whisper saying.

"May I help you?"

"Leyton, snap out of it!" Mr. Tysmens yelled.

"Yes, Mr. Tysmens."

"Sarah is asking you what you want," he replied.

"Yes, I would like strawberry ice cream with strawberry syrup and extra wet walnuts, please." She smiled with her eyes.

Mr. Tysmens said, "I would like the same."

She nods her head. "That's two," she said.

"Leyton, let's take a seat. When is your dad coming home?"

"It's looking like 2012, but I don't know."

"Leyton, does your mom or you need anything? Please, let me know. I am here for you."

"Thank you, Mr. Tysmens." I replied.

"Excuse me gentlemen. I hope you enjoy!"

"Thank you, Ms. Sarah."

While, we ate our ice cream, I could see on Mr. Tysmens face that he was thinking about something special to him. A smirk of a smile would come across his face. He would hold the spoon slightly over the ice cream sundae and stare in to the distance.

"What are you thinking about Mr.Tysmens?" I asked.

"Leyton, I was thinking about my son. I did not do these things with my son, when he was a boy. I made a lot of mistakes with my son. It was your dad who helped me to see that with you. I will always be grateful to your dad for that."

His smile was of a distance memory.

"My dad did that for you Mr. Tysmens?"

"Yes, he did!"

"Leyton, your dad is such a hero."

"How!?" I asked in excitement.

"Well, this story is going to have to take some time. My son's name is Averret. He was born premature. This means when a baby is born early, not fully developed or have health problems. My wife Beauty was beautiful. We thought we couldn't have kids. After ten years of trying, we gave up, out of the blue, Beauty was sick for days. She couldn't keep nothing on her stomach. We thought it was a stomach virus. I took her to the doctor. We were surprised when the doctor said she was pregnant. We thought he was joking. Averret was a reality. I still remember when she started showing her baby bump. The community was so excited. People was buying things for our son and storing it away. Averret was so blessed that we did not have to buy anything until he was two years old."

Mr. Tysmens telling me this story of their baby shower. It sounded so unreal. It was real. "We had four cars follow us home to help Beauty and I put all that baby stuff away. Your mom and dad was one of those four cars."

I smiled as I remembered as a little boy, "Dad, what are you smiling about? When you do that you are remembering something," said L.J.

This son of mine has learned to read his father so well. I couldn't do anything in front of him. I'm grateful that Mr. Tysmens took time with me when my dad was stationed off to wherever.

"L.J., I was thinking about Mr. Tysmens." I replied.

"Well, dad let's find Mr. Tysmen."

"Son, that is a good idea. We will go and look for him tomorrow, if it's God's will."

We stayed at my mom's and dad's old house. My parents gave it to me when they both decided not to come back to live. That two-story house was run down by the time I came back to it. It was the best investment to renovate that house. This is a vacation house without a mortgage. My wife and I don't have to drive far to the beach and get plenty of family time. When we got to the house, my wife was sitting on the back deck of the house listening to some jazz. You could see the relaxation over her body. L.J went to his room. I was trying to decide should I make a move. She looked too relax to zone out. I went upstairs and took a shower and ready for bed. I knew L.J. will be ready to go find Mr. Tysmens. Inside I am excited to see if this man is alive.

Chapter Two

In the morning, I woke up excited to find Mr. Tysmens. I looked at the clock, it was 7:10 a.m. I knew I had a little time to relax. I have so much to thank him for being that father figure to me when my father was away. Then I heard a knock on my bedroom door. "L.J. go away, it's too early in the morning," murmured my wife. I just chuckled.

"Come in, L.J." I said.

"Dad, I cooked breakfast. I have been looking on the internet last night for anyone with Tysmens. The coolest thing is I think I found Averret. If it is Averret Tysmens, we don't have to go far."

I got out of the bed, threw on my robe and walked downstairs. "What do you mean you think you found Averret Tysmens." What I didn't tell L.J. was Averret and I crossed paths while we were in the military. I knew I would find him. I just did not want too just yet. "Show me what you found, son."

L.J. grabs his laptop off the kitchen counter and brings it over to the breakfast nook. Before he opens the laptop, I knew it was going to be Averret. I did not think he was staying in his parent's house down the street. L.J. opens the laptop, pulls up the screen, show 'nough it was Averret. He was married with kids. Wow! This is telling me how old I am getting. I went to make me a cup of coffee. "Dad, how far is Mr. Tysmens' house used to be from here?"

That is when I remembered, I can't remember exactly which house or street it was. "L.J., I can't remember because I was still a little boy, a little younger than your age."

"Dad, do you think this is Averret?" He asked.

"Son, I think that is Averret." In my mind I don't know if Averret will remember me. I am going to play it safe. We have something else in common that we both probably would like to forget. It changed us for the better, we don't take things for granted after that night. L.J. and I ate our breakfast, talked and thought of places where the older people would hanged out to see if they knew where we could find Averret or Mr. Tysmens. We made a list of three places. I looked at the time, it was almost 8:00 a.m. I remembered that these old men chill out and talk about the good ole days at the Lilly's Bistro. They mostly go there to get a cup of coffee, a biscuit, fellowship and see the people in the town. It is their way of keeping up with what is going on in town. We got dressed and hopped in the car. Before I put the car in reverse, we looked at each other, paused and said, "MOM." L.J. grabs his phone and send a text to let her know we left the house. She has a pet peeve about us leaving the house and not telling her. We understand why because we are African American males. When L.J. sent the text, we sighed, the first place we agreed on was going to Lilly's. We rode up and I saw Mr. Roadder. He was the Post Master at the post office for years. It's funny seeing him all old now. I parked the car, jumped out to catch up him before he got in his car. "Mr. Roadder, Mr. Roadder!" I yelled.

He stops to look at who is calling him. He sees me from a distance. His face was looking to remember who I was. "Do you remember Mr. Tysmens having a little boy with him while his dad was stationed away?"

His eyes got so big. In his weak, but yet strong voice, "Leyton!"

He hugged me so tight. "I often thought about you and your mother after y'all left Loeville."

We caught up. It seem like we talked for hours, but it was just thirty minutes. L.J. was enjoying the conversation. I asked Mr. Roadder if he know where is Mr. Tysmens now. He put his head down. "He is at the "La'View"." He said it was an assist living facility where he had his own apartment, near a golf course and shops. He moved there right after Beauty passed away. He couldn't handle it. Averret and his family stays there when they come to visit.

Mr. Roadder face lit up like a Christmas tree. "You know what?!" He exclaimed. "Averret is here now. He got here yesterday afternoon." He said.

"Oh! Really!" L.J. looks at me like we got confirmation. "Mr. Roadder, what street was Mr. Tysmen's house?" I asked.

He paused to think. "I believe it was Potters Street. It was 214 Potters Street because Ms. Beaman's house the librarian was best friend with Beauty. Well, Leyton glad to see you again. Nice meeting your son, L.J. I have to get ready to ride into town for a doctor's appointment." He shook my hand and got into the car. L.J. and I stood there looking at each other just smiling.

"Dad, one stop shop." said L.J.

"Just one."

Chapter Three

We didn't want to go to someone's house this early in the morning. We did ride to see what 214 Potter Street looks like now. It didn't look like what I remembered. We rode back to the house. My wife was sitting in the kitchen drinking a cup of coffee and eating one of her breakfast sandwiches. I gave her a kiss on the forehead, L.J. gave her a kiss on the cheek. She smiles.

"Where have you two been early this morning?" She asked. L.J. and I look at each other and laugh.

"Mom, you talk in your sleep. We have told you so many times. You aren't listening when we tell you. You insisted," chuckled L.J.

"L.J. shut up and tell me again." She replied.

"Babe, L.J. found Mr. Tysmens's son Averret. He lives in Mr. Tysmens old house around the corner from us. Mr. Tysmens lives in this assistant living with his own apartment. Mr. Roadder who is the old Post Master of the post office gave me all this information this morning. It was funny to L.J. and I that we did not get to walk into Lilly's. We got everything we needed in the parking lot with Mr. Roadder."

"That is good, babe. Are you going to see Averret? Enough time has passed now since all of that. I would love to see Ashleigh." She smiled while putting her dishes away in the dishwasher.

"Are you telling me you want to go with L.J. and I to see Averret?" asked Leyton.

"Yes," she replied.

"Fine, Le Tina." She walked out of the kitchen going upstairs with a bounce in her step. She smiled all the way up the stairs. I didn't want to look at L.J. because I could feel this confused look on his face.

"Dad, you already knew Averret Tysmens. Why you didn't tell me?" asked L.J.

I took a deep breath. "L.J., what I didn't explain is that our paths crossed in the military. I don't want to go into any more details."

L.J. gaved me a look of hurt and confusion. He went upstairs to his room. I knew I had messed up again by lying to my son. I didn't want to deal or talk about the real issue that is behind Averret and my friendship.

Tina comes downstairs looking at me with this frustrated face. I already knew what it was.

"Why did you lie to L.J. about Averret?" She asked. She took a deep breath and paused. "Carl and Charlesten," she said. She walked away. She turns around. "Leyton, you have to deal with this. I thought you had healed. I see you haven't because you would have told L.J. the truth about Averret. Your son is feeling like a fool. You know you have to make this right. You hurt our son. He is really messed up over this."

She walked away and went upstairs looking at me until she couldn't any longer. I stood there in the kitchen what seemed like for hours. Yes, I know where Mr. Tysmens is now. I have to find the piece to my healing before I see Averret. I grab L.J.'s laptop. I begin to search for Charlesten's family. For the first time, I begin to cry.

Chapter Four

I didn't know what to do. I couldn't find Charlesten's family members. I tried to look for his aunt and his uncle. I couldn't find anyone who look similar to them. I went to La View. I drove up to the gate. The speaker said, "Hello. How may I help you?" I look around the property. This was some high-tech assist living quarters. "I am here to see Mr. Tysmen."

The speaker said, "Please drive to the main office." The gate lifted on the right side. I drove through the gate. I read the signs to the main office. It looked like a business office in a nook on a Hawaiian beach. It looked so relaxing. It had a small lake to look at while you sit in the waiting area. I walked in the door. It was small but spacious. The young girl smiled at me. "Sir, what is your name?"

"My name is Leyton Peyton." I don't think it was five minutes but I saw a golf cart running so fast that it looks as if it was about to tip over coming around the corner. I was laughing but scared at the same time. It was Mr. Tysmen. I heard some of the other neighbors screamed, "LOU! SLOW DOWN!"

Lou hit the brakes. The cart stopped an inch away from hitting the building. The young girl that welcomed me said, "Mr. Louis, what have I told you about this?"

"Yea, Yea. I get points because I didn't hit the building this time." He replied.

"Mr. Louis, that isn't the point. Enjoy your company, we will talk later."

"Thank you."

Mr. Tysmens voice is just as I remember it but now a little raspy because he was older. He didn't look his age.

"You want to go back to my place?" He asked.

"Only if I can drive the cart." I replied. He laughed so hard until he coughs.

"Leyton, you have not change. You still have that smart funny little boy that I would spend my Saturday and sometimes Sundays. Your mother wouldn't let you come to me if I spent all day Saturday with you. She said, "I needed a break." Leyton you were a handful plus, you were preparing me for when Averret came back into my life. I will be forever grateful for what you did for him before you left the Army."

Mr. Tysmen knew about Carl and Charlesten. I just paused in my walking, smiled and the tears just started to flow. Mr. Tysmens walked me out of the office. I got on the cart. Mr. Tysmens drove the correct way. We got to his townhouse/condo. He pushed me in the door. He made me sit down.

"Have you seen Averret yet?" He asked.

"No," I said.

"Please go see him. He is staying in at the house. He uses it as a vacation house. He will be leaving in a few days."

"Few days," I shouted.

"Yes," replied Mr. Tysmens.

Mr. Tysmens picked up the phone. He walked outside on his patio. He stayed outside for a while. I didn't think it was Averret on the phone. This place was beautiful and calming. It makes you feel like you are on a resort instead of an assist living. I just sat there and looked around. He had a view of the lake and the golf course. The sunsets by the lake. That is an awesome place to reflect for the day. I got so comfortable that I must have dozed off. I didn't realize it. When I came to myself, Mr. Tysmens was prepping food as if we were about to have a cookout. "Who is all this food for, Mr. Tysmens?" I asked.

"You'll see, Leyton," he replied. He continue to put the food in a cooler on the back of the golf cart. He was humming some song, that sounded familiar but I couldn't remember. I began to help to put the food in the cooler.

"Put it down, Leyton. Now!" said Mr. Tysmens sternly.

I walked away and went to sit down in the living room. I didn't know what to do with myself. I really didn't. I am usually doing something to help, packing or something. A memory came to me when I was in the military. Colonel Boveins pulled this prank on me. I learned my lesson to learn to ask for help. It didn't have to be done the way I wanted, but get it done in excellence. Another lesson just came in, ask and if the person says no then you have to respect that. Don't push, let them reach out to you. You just have to be there when they ask. I heard Mr. Tysmens shouting out my name. "Leyton, Leyton lets go."

I get on the golf car. He drove like he had sense again. I was amazed. The people in the community was looking and standing in awe when they saw him coming through. We got to the outdoor kitchen/patio. I saw Tina, L.J., Averret and his family, and three other people. What did Mr. Tysmens do? I began to take some of the food out of the cooler. Tina walked towards me. She grabbed my hand to move away from everyone. She gently rubbed my face.

"Babe, you have been crying."

"Yes," I replied. I didn't want to admit it. "That night will always be a part of me. I can't let it take control over me. It's a way for me to help someone to overcome like I will."

Tina smiled, "You are ready to get therapy now."

"Yes," I said.

"Your healing is going to begin tonight," she said. She pointed to the three people that I don't know who they were. "This is Carl's sister and Charlesten's two brothers. You are going to help them to get closure as well."

The tears begin to flow like a river. Tina grabbed me to hold me and reminded me to breathe. She took me in the building to the bathroom. She talked me down from my emotions. She wiped my face, then walked me through the steps of taking deep breaths. Once I was calm, we went back to the patio. Averret didn't say anything but gave me a hug. He whispered in my ear, "Thank you."

When he said that, I couldn't let him go just yet. He didn't know how much I needed to hear that from him. Tina stood by watching and making sure I didn't break down. I didn't! I whispered in his ear, "I needed that. I blamed myself for so long."

Averret let me go. He walked me over to a bench near the lake. We sat down. He put his hand around my neck. "You saved my life that night. You saw that Carl was suicidal. You saw all the signs. We didn't want to see it because Carl was the guy that was just wild out. He tricked Charlesten that night. We lost two that night. I would've been in the car too if you hadn't invited me to go with you. I met my wife because of you. I have a family because of you. My Dad would have been mourning my death as well if I didn't listen. I wouldn't experience being a father, husband and traveling the world because of you. The biggest thing you introduce me to was God. He is the best friend that I have ever known. I understand what that means now. If God takes my dad home tonight, I would be hurt but I know I can make it because God is on my side. Most of all I am in His will. When I am not in His will, things goes out of sync. Then there are times when it is just the enemy that doesn't want you to do God's work. I am determined after loss of not just one friend, but two good friends. I am alive for a reason. I look for that reason each day."

For the first time, I felt free. It is undescribed form of freedom that I haven't felt before. I believe this is what it means in church, where they say you have a freedom that can't be described, a joy that can't be explained, and a peace beyond understanding. I couldn't say a word but cry. While I cried, Averret prayed so many different prayers. Each prayer was something that I had been feeling but free from now. As our families and friends continued to do fellowship and mingle, I was experiencing a true process.

Chapter Five

I thought I was about done with the process. I was just staring into the view of the lake. I saw Mr. Tysmens walking over near Averret. He gave his son a hug. "Did you tell him yet?" asked Mr. Tysmens.

"No, Dad. He needed to be free first." Averret replied.

"He has that bond with guilt and the mind games."

"Yes, Dad," said Averret.

Averret got up from the bench. "Son, leave us alone for a while," said Mr. Tysmens. Averret knotted his head and walked away. Mr. Tysmens started talking, "Don't say a word. Just listen. You had to save my son that night because we weren't speaking at the time. His mother was our bridge of communication. She was the one who balanced us out. She knew about Averret dabbing into homosexuality. I don't believe in that. The Bible says that a man and a woman multiply. I realized that he found himself in his mother more than in me. I didn't teach or build him up to be a man. When he got into the Army, I saw a boy turn into a man. Beauty would tell me but I would brush it off. Let me see it for myself. Beauty didn't tell me or Averret that she was sick. Her death was a complete shock. If it wasn't for you being obedient and telling my son to come with you that night, I don't know how would I handle losing my wife and son in less than ten years. I might have been an alcoholic or on drugs. I don't know, but I am grateful to the little boy who followed me and taught me how to be a father. When Averret did come home, I had to learn how to be a father to a man, not a little boy. I knew within him was a little boy who wanted his dad, just like you Leyton."

We both laughed. I have done so much good. The good that I was feeling was like I wasn't doing anything. God let me know I had done something greater than anyone could imagine. I kept a father from losing his son. God allowed me to put a father and son relationship back together. "You served your country well before you retired. You will learn more once you get yourself together," said Mr. Tysmen. He walked away. I sat there in awe. I sat there hoping that my head will not turn this to being a dream. It wasn't! This was the reality of what I was hoping that being a servant is hard work. The benefits are worth every piece of satisfaction to your soul.

Chapter Six

My mind didn't know where to go next. I was smiling while tears continued to fall down my face. I didn't know what to think. I look to the left of me, I saw Carl's sister and Charlesten's two brothers coming towards me. One of the brothers had a beach chair to make sure he could sit down. I chuckled to myself. When I look again at Carl's sister, she was right there in front of me. "My name is Da'Kesha. You can call me Kesha," she said.

"Hello Kesha." I replied.

"Let me just say thank you. I know you tried to save my brother. It was when he was thirteen, he went to stay at one of our uncle's houses in the country one summer. I went to my aunt, my mom's sister and stayed the summer there. When we came back home a week before school started, Carl was wild, acting out, cursing at mom and angry. It was our first time staying for the summer. It wasn't Carl's first time being with our uncle. His son Drew would come over, Carl and Drew was inseparable. That summer Carl never told mom and I what happened. Sir, it wasn't his first time trying to commit suicide. The first-time mom and I was coming from a road trip, he didn't want to go. He stayed home. Mom had my aunt and our cousin to check on him before and after they got off work. Mom and I could have done the road trip in one day. We wanted to take our time and enjoy the scenery. We came home. Carl was in the middle of the bathroom floor unresponsive, with a half-bottle of Vodka and prescription pills bottle empty. The EMTs said we had gotten there just in time. If a minute later, I wouldn't have my brother. My mom tried to put him in therapy. He didn't want to go to therapy. My mom enforced that he goes. He was doing better. It was like I had my old Carl back. Mysteriously, his junior year of high school, my freshman year of high school, we went to wake mom up to let her know something we needed for school. Mom wouldn't wake up. Carl was the one who found her. I guess that was the hump that broke the camel's back. Carl stayed off the tracks. It was by the grace of God that he graduated high school. My aunt which was our dad's older sister became our guardians. She did the best she could. Then she got married to Steve. Carl calm down a lot. A year after he got in the Army, Steve got sick. It put him in a wheel chair. Carl behavior was so off the chain. My aunt had to call the police on Carl. It was the night he died. He called and told me everything that happened at our uncle's house. He told where to get proof of the video. We put our uncle in jail. My uncle was in a child porn ring. He kept that thing under wraps. NO ONE knew. He didn't tell the therapist. She would tell my mom she was working on trying to get Carl to open up. He was an air tight volt. The therapist did tell my mom that a client left their cigarette lighter in the chair. Carl stared at it for so long she was worried. When he picks it up from the seat, she almost had to pull it from his hand. This gave Mom the answer that the scars on his back was from being burned. They were first degree burns. Mom cried for days. I believe that is what killed her because she started investigating and she was angry with herself that she put her son in that situation. I had to think who knew! No one in the family knew until the police revealed it to us. The police had been watching him for over two years. They became suspicious when they saw Carl with him that summer."

The tears rolling down her face was making my heart ache for her. Charlesten's brothers put their arms around her. While wiping their tears and hers. I realize I gave her more time with Carl. He finally told her the truth. He couldn't handle the pain of seeing that being over the black market.

"Carl told me the reason this boy name Chris was bullying him in school because he found out about the child porn material he did with his uncle," said Kesha.

I took a deep breath. "Kesha, how did Chris learn of this? He didn't need to know nothing about that underworld."

Tears still flowing, she said, "His dad was one of the top drug dealers in the area. He finally got caught. The police in our area couldn't touch him because majority of them had some dirt that would destroy their home or career."

I looked at Kesha with a straight face. I said, "I served a country that couldn't get drug dealers off the streets. Because they couldn't have any character." With a voice of anger, I was upset. "When directors and writers create these movies, there is some truth behind these stories."

Kesha leans over to rub my back. "Calm down, Le'. It's just that real."

I heard Mr. Tysmens calling for us to eat. I was too upset to eat. I wanted to fight. I didn't know the rest of the story. Mr. Tysmens walked over. He must felt the tension. Kesha nodded her head. Mr. Tysemens said, "Let's go!"

Chapter Seven

Mr. Tysmens and I went for a walk around the path of the lake. Tears were still running down my face. I didn't have any control over them. I was releasing everything I was feeling. I just came to the realization that it will stop when it was time. I continued to inhale and exhale as we walked. It was silence for about a third of the walk.

"God don't make no mistakes, Leyton," said Mr. Tysmens. I let out this painful scream that made me fall to my knees. Mr. Tysmens made sure we weren't in view of everyone at the outdoor kitchen. He let me weep, get in a ball, air punch, everything that would allow me to release this feeling of pain. "You are not taking this back home with you, Leyton." He said in a firm, caring voice. I knew he really cared and it seem as if I cried harder. I knew I had to get myself together. Charlesten's brothers need to talk to me. I need to hear what they had to say. As I was kicking, silently screaming from the memory of the day, I saw that car being pulled from the river. I walked away because I didn't want to see their bodies. Then I was the one who had to identify both of them because I was their sergeant in the US Army. I reported them missing because I knew already that Carl had done this. Why no one listens to me? Then I heard a voice say inside me say "one". I stop, jump and look around to see if I would hear it again. I did not see anyone around Mr. Tysmens and I. I said out loud, "Say it again."

The voice was so still, calm, soft but louder this time. It said, "One." I looked again, no one was around but Mr. Tysmens and I. I dust myself off, went to the bathrooms near the front office to wash my face and put myself back together. The voice I heard was the Holy Spirit. I have been told many stories of God. I experienced it for myself that day, second and moment. I walk out of that bathroom refreshed, like I had a shower. Mr. Tysmens looked at me with a smile. "God didn't want you to wallow in that pain anymore. You got the message. IF you save one, you completed the mission," said Mr. Tysmens with a chuckle in his voice. He patted me on the back. We walked around the other side where we could begin to see the outdoor kitchen. Everyone began to cheer for me like it was a graduation. I laugh because it was my graduation from moving on from this piece of the past. I didn't carry that anymore. My mission was "one".

Chapter Eight

Mr. Tysmens and everyone began to clap and cheer harder. All I could do is smile. My cheeks are beginning to hurt. They hurt so much tears were forming in my eyes. When my L.J. saw that one tear run down my face, he came next to me to hold my hand. I grab his head to kiss him on the forehead. In this day and time, someone would say this is gay. Affection don't have to be gay or lesbianism, or as military don't have to be hard most of the time. We are human. We can be exactly who we are. That moment with my son let me know I can be who I am. In being who I am shows the real me. It doesn't matter if you like me or not. As I hear these cheers and hand claps, someone does like or love me for who I am. They started yelling, "SPEECH, SPEECH, SPEECH!"

I raised my hands to get their attention before I spoke. I opened my mouth, nothing came out. I knew why. I have anxiety. It was trying to show its head. I couldn't let this win today on a day that I was being celebrated. I know I deserve this honor. Averret is here because of God in me.

"Everyone, thank you for coming here to celebrate me. Thank you for your patience earlier. Today, I have learned a lot of things. We carry blame and others' responsibility, because someone didn't listen. Rejection comes to build us and make us stronger. Even if I was rejected, God let me know when I save one person. I did my job! I might want to save two or more people. When you are on the journey, it might not feel good but it is worth it. My family, friends and everyone that I helped, you are worth it."

We all clapped, cheered and disperse to their seats. As I sat there just looking at my surrounding, L.J. was smiling at me.

"What is it son?" I asked.

"Nothing, Dad. You are a hero. You act like you are not. You take your honor in such humbleness." He replied.

"Son, the Bible says, "the meek and humble shall inherit the earth." Another scripture is "Pride brings destruction". If I let pride in, then I can't appreciate the bigger things God wants to do for me. For me to get those things I have to be humble. Do you understand, son?"

L.J. was looking deep in thought that he just gave me the biggest hug. I couldn't let him go. It felt like the day I brought him home from the hospital. I couldn't put him down in the crib. I did! I saw the effects of a spoil child. He may be annoying at times, but he is one of the greatest gifts God has given me. "Yes, Dad, yes, I do," replied L.J.

Tina put our plates on the table. She was wiping tears from her eyes like the day she held L.J. for the first time. When I saw her still standing there. I grab her too. We all hugged up in a huddle. If I didn't get over this pain, we would not be having this moment. My family receives a new me today. This is what a fresh start looks and feel like with my family.

Chapter Nine

My family finally came out of the huddle. L.J. and I had to warm our food. The food was delicious. I was greedy when it came down to that pull pork. I don't know who cooked it. The seasoning was outrageous. It felt like I was going on a Southern adventure of the United States. When my mind went back to that sorrow and frustrated area of my life. I didn't realize I was wallowing in pain. I couldn't control it. I did what God wanted me to do. I saved one. This is what I was missing, my family seeing the good I have done. Most of all, God saw what I have done. I didn't understand why I was so blessed. I know now. I begin to smile. Tina gently lays her hand on my back. Her look was like I have not seen this man before.

"Le', you need to talk to Charleston's brothers. It's getting late."

"Yeah. It is but I am just not ready for what they have to tell me." I replied. Tina took a deep breath and gave me a kiss that electrified my heart. I had to remember where I was. I heard L.J. say, "Get a room."

"Thanks, son. Babe look for a room. We are going to leave L.J. with Mr. Tysmens, if that is ok. Find out while I talk to Charlesten's brothers." I said.

Tina smiled. I walked over to Charlesten's brothers. It felt like I was walking so slow. When I got to their table, I saw the brothers just happy and joyful I had made it to them.

"Hello gentlemen. What are your names? I am sorry I didn't get to talk to you until now. Thank you for being patient with me."

They smiled and nodded their head. "No problem, Sarg. You tried to save my brother. He was the kid who was hard headed. He wouldn't listen to nobody. He had to find out for himself. My name is Carlos, and he is Christian. We learned that we have a nephew. Charlesten got this girl pregnant. We knew that girl since she was a kid. She wasn't the type to go and sleep around. Charlesten wanted to be that player. The girl was in junior year of college. She didn't know how to get in contact with him. She contacted Carlos. Carlos still lives in the area we grew up. Her father knew where Carlos stayed. Carlos does car repair from his home as a side hustle. He is good. He should have his own business. He doesn't believe in himself like I do. Anyway, when Charlesten got the phone call from Carlos that evening, he was upset. He said the girl was lying. We knew the girl wasn't lying. We did the DNA test when the baby got here. The baby came out looking like Charlesten. We prayed for that spirit to be broken over this child. We didn't want another life lost."

They took a picture of the baby boy. "He has his eyes! What is his name?" I asked.

"His name is Charles Edward Lee."

"That is very strong name." I replied.

"Yes, it's from strong men. Lee was from your name. Edward is her grandfather's name. That man was awesome. I will tell you stories about him. He was so intelligent and wise. He would blow your mind with things. The Pastors and ministers in the area would visit him when they had issues and problems. He lived to be a hundred and five years old."

"Christian is the talkative one. I am not. I want to say thank you."

When Carlos said that, I felt something that was so genuine and pure. I begin to cry again. When I did, Carlos just gave me a hug. He whispered in my ear. "You can't save everyone. If they listen and take heed. They can be saved."

I breathe and cried, just in that pattern. Until, I was able get a grip on my emotions. Christian and Carlos gave me their numbers and addresses so I can visit and call Charles. They call him C.E.L aka Cel. It's 9:15 p.m. at night, everyone was starting to leave. The night air was starting to get chilly. Everyone helped clean up, gave us hugs and kisses as they left.

Mr. Tysmens allowed L.J. to stay with him the next two nights. Those two nights, I made it up to my wife. I was the grown man that she was wondering where he was. After that one day, I was changed forever. L.J. kept saying when he came home. Where is my dad? Who are you? All I could do was laugh, because he was seeing someone I would not allow no one to see but God.

God wanted me to be free. I just didn't know how. That is what I see with so many people today. No one knows how to be free. We say we are free but looking at the world, the laws and more, it is scary that we are free to a certain extend only. The only place where we are free is in the presence of God. God presence is the best place to be. I don't discuss this with a lot of people, due to the fact that you must have spiritual eyes to see this beauty.

Chapter Ten

I received a call from my friend, Ron. Ron is that friend who is cool and loving. He stays right by your side. When it came to the ladies, Ron was a garden tool. Yep! That is what I meant. I meant what I said. Close to a half a century, but he still doesn't know what a wife is. He was content being single. There are some people who won't allow themselves to be delivered from their past. Ron is one of those people. They have so much to offer the world. They won't allow themselves to be open to accept the world in. He is too afraid to be hurt, harmed or feel the brokenness so he can be healed. Ron had the opportunity to be a Colonel before he retired from the Army. He didn't want to the work. He wants to be enlisted for another four or eight years. I understood. We saw things coming that we see that is taking place today.

Anyway, Ron calls for two things, they are to check in or to inform you. This call was for both. He wanted to let me know that one of the privates was killed. It is a homicide. This young man was one of the ones we didn't have to worry about. He had an awesome heart. He enjoyed helping others. Ron let me know he was shot in the head from behind. It was skilled shot like an assassin. After I got off the phone with Ron. I cried much harder. I knew this boy's mother was heartbroken. He was like a son to Ron and I. Ron is going to keep me informed when the funeral or memorial service will be. It won't be an open casket because his face was dismantled. I stood in the middle of my living room. Tina and L.J was coming down stairs laughing, talking, they both stopped on the stairs. They saw I was crying. When Tina hugged me, I just broke down. Tina was trying to find out what was wrong. I couldn't talk. She found my phone. She saw that Ron had called. She called Ron back. He told her what he told me. When she heard it. She screamed and dropped the phone. We loved the kid like our own. He would even baby sit L.J. for us to have a break when we were having trouble in our marriage. He was an angel for real. He is gone too soon. His name was Corporal Christopher Lee Is' ghee.

This was the first time L.J. was standing in the middle of his parents being heartbroken. It was nothing he could do but watch, pray and console us.

Chapter Eleven

In the next few days, Tina and I went to the funeral. L.J. stayed with Mr. Tysmens while we were out of state. We didn't like why we were going back to Virginia because it is a sad occasion. We were enjoying our time together as well as looking forward to seeing everyone. Especially, Peter and Chrissy. They are one couple who will keep you laughing. Christopher hanged around them a lot too. He would stay overnight or even would come stay if he was too tired to drive home sometimes. He had his own room, seriously. We are going to stay with Peter and Chrissy while we are here. Ron let us know he was going to come by once he was in Virginia. The reunion started at five o'clock that evening, when we got out of the car. Peter and Chrissy met us in the driveway. We hugged each other so tight. We didn't want to let each other go. Peter and Leyton watched us for a while. They knew, but words weren't needed at this time. It was just that physical contact. Even though Chrissy and I was crying silently. We caught Leyton and Peter looking at each other like in awe. They were so glad to see each other. They sat on the porch while Chrissy and I was on the back deck sitting in silence. Chrissy said, "He was at the house over a week ago. He was sleepy. He couldn't drive home because his eyes were so heavy. He made it to the couch. Chris slept there over three hours. You know how loud Peter and the kids get when we speak on the phone. Tina, he didn't even move or heard a sound. I felt something wrong but I couldn't put my finger on it. I told Peter to talk to him. He did, but Christopher wouldn't talk. I wish he would've. I believe he was helping someone. It was too much for him."

Tina leaned over to place my hand on her hand. We watched the sunset, while sipping on our drinks. Almost eight o'clock that night, Ron pulls up in the driveway, hitting his horn on the car. We all laughed, because that was our cue. Ron was here. The party is getting ready to get started. The surprise was he had a female in the car. She looked like us. She was an African American, maybe in her late thirties. We spot a ring on her hand. Chrissy and Tina played it cool. We all greeted her and Ron.

"Surprise! Meet Mrs. Gracie Phee Williams!" shouts Ron. We all stood like what. We couldn't move. We were shocked. We knew Ron was a garden tool. He worked that profession so well. We wiped the shocked off our faces. We greeted her with open arms. We fixed her a drink, sat on the back deck while the men were in the house. All three was in the man cave down stairs in the basement. Gracie started talking, she was cool. She told us that Ron was a hoe. She knew what she had on her plate. She let us know she recognized a hoe when you are one yourself. She had started to change her ways. Her children were grown. She didn't have any responsibilities. She met a guy and he used her. She was done. A friend invited her to come to a party at the "Pavillion". It is country club near the Naval base.

"I didn't want to go that night. It was a Friday night." She continued to tell the story, telling us that as she sat at the table. She did not want to drink. She was just going to show her face in the place then disappear for the night. "Before I could do that. Ron comes to sit at the table. I knew he wanted a booty call. Ron asked me to dance, I did."

"I knew what Ron was looking for I didn't give him the time of day. After a few dances on the floor, I left and came home. Ron asked for my number. I told him no. I went home and continued with my life. I am a social worker. He found me. It was exactly three months later. He took me to lunch. I couldn't get rid of him. It was six months later he put a ring on my hand. I still sit in awe of this ring being on my hand. We had a small ceremony at his sister Stacey's house. We had our honeymoon in Ocean City, Maryland. It was beautiful watching the sunset that whole week." This is how we became five to six. Tina looked at me. "You are the woman for him." We told her. The ladies don't tell Ron no because he is so handsome and smooth. They want to get with him so bad. The woman you are going to marry is going to tell you no. She is going to stick to her answer. If you try to push her over, you wish you have not pushed at all.

We all begin to laugh. She said, "Yes, he tried. After what I did. He wishes he didn't."

He is very intelligent, even though he doesn't act like it at times. The night ended in laughs and more laughs. Until, we couldn't say good night. It was later.

Chapter Twelve

The day of the funeral, we felt so heavy. Chrissy was crying before we could even leave the house. Leyton was in the shower crying. Peter was keeping himself busy with anything that hide his emotions or keep from crying. Chris was like a son but most of all a friend we trust. Chris was that friend if we were doing something wrong, he was going to let you know it was wrong. It would go to his grave with him. I know all of us have something we are grateful to him that it is gone together with him. That morning was a mess. All six of us went in two by two. We left that service two by two. Peter and Chrissy's backyard was our place for the rest of that day.

Tina looked at Chrissy with the words "that sound", those words meant a lot. Christopher's mother was weeping and yelling during the service when the family started talking about the last family events he spent time with them. Christopher closest cousin name was Brody. Brody was adopted by Christopher's aunt and uncle in the late 90's. Brody wouldn't talk hardly. He would speak to his aunt and uncle. That was with yes, sir, no, sir, yes, ma'am, etc.

Brody wouldn't have a conversation with no one. One day, his aunt and uncle came home for the holidays. Brody saw Christopher's collection of GI Joe's and Transformers. He lite up! Brody talked to Christopher. That is what made his aunt and uncle move closer to home so they could spend more time together. It was the best days when they played high school football. Brody attended Northwest High School. Chris attended Western High School. When these two schools would play each other, you would think it was Duke vs. UNC-Chapel Hill. The school colors were similar. You had to identify if you were with the colors you wore or your words. Brody and Christopher would have their personal bet that one of their classmates would figured out. They thought it was cool. Then the whole team started to participate in the bet. Brody and Christopher could start paying someone to cut their parents' grass. Both of their parents had big yards.

The hardest day was when Christopher went off to basic training. Chris and Brody talk, laugh and cried for weeks. They were so happy for each other. Brody had gotten a scholarship to play for Albany State University. It is known to be dirty south of Georgia. You had to know how to survive the heat during the summer. It was the dirty, dirty, dirty, south. Brody was doing so good that the coach gave Brody his real time on the field. Brody did so good. The coach started making Brody his secret weapon. Chris surprised Brody one time by coming to his game. Brody thought he saw Chris but shook it off. The coach told Brody that he saw something different that night that he had not seen in him before. Brody told the coach I thought I saw my cousin and best friend Chris. The coach said you did. When Chris walked into that locker room. The coach cried with them. Brody and Chris relationship was an example of true brotherhood.

"The time he would come see me play were the best. Chris would tell me what he saw on the field. It was because of Brody that I learned to play every position on the field except one. This is what got me signed to the pros. I am forever grateful. I will take care of aunty for you. If it was me Chris, you would do the same for me." Brody placed the transformer on the casket and walked away with tears running down his face holding on to the memory of what was.

Peter got Brody's phone number before the procession left. We couldn't handle the repast. The backyard spoke for us. We saw Chris everywhere. A piece of him was poking at each of us in some way or another. The silence of our souls were crying for Chris, Oh! Chris!

Chapter Thirteen

The days after Chris funeral was the hardest. Tina was functional but not productive. Chrissy was just moving. Peter wouldn't even say his name. Ron was the one who was handling it. Brody did call for our help. We had to do a group therapy call all together because we understood. The hardest part was the investigation of who or what happened to Chris just came to a holt. This is what made all of us angry and frustrated. Chris deserves justice. Chris's mother deserves closure. We begin to learn that closure doesn't come easy. It's like a person who has been through a divorce. You might not ever get any closure. You will get peace, that is better than closure. I have learned that through life's friendships and relationships.

Chris death has given me another point of view of life. I can't explain it. I know that I can't do nothing. I am going to speak to the police officer or detective on the case. No one has found his phone. Chris phone is missing. Whoever it was that killed him, it was connected to that phone. Is it possible that someone could send out a signal for his phone? I believe his phone is the clue. I send a prayer request to our people of God and the local Chaplin.

Chapter Fourteen

I called Chris' mother. I told her the plan of letting the people of God to pray that the phone will be found. God can do the impossible. I haven't slept a full night of sleep since Chris has died. I won't be able to sleep until I know that phone is found. She was fine with it. She said "the power of prayer". We began to inform churches and other organizations that has prayer meetings. The first month we saw things happening. The detective would have small led to what happen that night, such as the footage of the parking lot was more visible. Someone gave a statement about seeing Chris at this girl house. He was helping her with a situation. The person gave the name of the hotel. The information was still on record. We were thanking God for anything he would give us. The tips begin to slow down. It was a month. Two. Three. It was six months and no led or tips on Chris case. We didn't stop praying. We knew God is going to reveal the truth. God knows everything. He told Job that he was smarter than any man. When I would get discouraged, I would read that conversation between Job and God. I didn't know best, but God did. I still continued with life.

I didn't give up on my family. I didn't shut them out. I almost did at a point when I went into a depression. I didn't tell Tina about what I was feeling. God must let her know. She pulled me out of it. I am grateful. I continued to join the local prayer groups. I even hosted some at my home. Chris deserved justice. Then one day during prayer group a young lady who was new. I didn't know her. She said, "God said the girl will be found soon. I will reveal the answers to everything." It was almost a year since Chris's death. When God says soon, his soon is not our version of soon. God soon can be a day, months, weeks or years.

I prayed each night reminding God what he said. L.J. would pray with me sometimes. We all had faith that we would find the answer to Chris death. He was a good young man. I would want someone to seek justice if it was L.J. Chris was my other son. Ron made me mad how he functioned thru this pain. I understood even more what the elderly meant "if it wasn't for the Lord who was on my side, where would I'd be". God showed me so many things that the conversation with Job in the Bible was so important. Proverbs 4:13 says, "Keep her, for she is your life." Wisdom will keep your life. It takes wisdom to live in this life. Knowledge is the other part that works with wisdom. You don't have to let others know what knowledge and wisdom you have. You give unto to what God says you shall release. As I would continue to read and study God's word. God would give me the simplest things which was so profound. It was scary, funny and heavy all in one. It was that moment I knew God was changing me. I like this change and Tina did too.

Chapter Fifteen

Today makes two years since Chris death. I was hoping that we would have an answer by now. We all were still praying. It slowed down a little. I knew people would get tired. I couldn't get tired or lose hope. I expect something every day. I would look at the news on television and the internet. I searched high and low. Tina and I started having Chris mom come stay with us for the holidays. We wanted her to come and move to North Carolina. She wouldn't, but we are still trying. Brody was taking care of her as well. Between Tina, myself, Brody and Ron, she was taken care of.

We all would have a group call around the anniversary of Chris's death. It made me feel good that they supported me in the prayer group. They were glad that I didn't go on the hunt myself. Something could have happened to me. As we continue with the call, we tell each other we love them. It was so touching. Men expressing how we feel about each other isn't guy friendly. Chris' death made us all even much softer in spirit. We never thought we would be so sensitive during our late fifties almost sixty years old. Chris isn't going to experience getting old, married, kids and all the things God has given us. Tina started crying so hard she was weeping on the phone. The guys got silent. All I could do is hold Tina. She would pick at Chris because he wasn't the type of guy that knew how to approach women. He would call Tina for advice. He was comfortable talking to her about things like that. Chrissy was the mom figure where he knew he could relax, clear his head and regroup. Peter wouldn't say a word still. I couldn't go and let him keep holding this in. "Peter, let it go. Scream, cry, tell God you are angry if you are for taking Chris. You have to stop holding this in."

It was then that the biggest tears fell from his eyes. I have never seen Peter cry. Ron said, "Let it out, man. It isn't healthy for you. It isn't fair to Chrissy either."

At that moment, Peter let out a yell that cut us so deep that we cried too. We wanted to hug him but couldn't through video. Chrissy was holding him so tight. She was being there for her husband. We stayed on the video call for a little while longer but we soon gave Peter his privacy. Peter was the private one. It was like two weeks we didn't here from Peter and Chrissy. Chrissy cleared their schedules for a week. During that week, Chrissy allowed Peter to just express his grief for Chris. He had been holding it in for two years. It was past due for him to release this grief. I learned from Peter later on, like months to a year later. He broke things, screamed, sat in silence and cried, and had sex with Chrissy. He explains that the sex wasn't the normal love making. It wasn't an intense heat of the moment or because they were desiring each other. It was so sensual. He wouldn't allow Chrissy to wear nothing but a robe. He explained that he was not going to do anything to hurt her. He needed to release to feel good afterwards. It wasn't going to be a good feeling like high. It was going to be a release of the next level of grief. The first morning early before the break of day, Peter explained how he just smelled Chrissy hair. The night before she washed in the Dove's Pink Rose body wash. He just smelled, studied her body, and laid his body on her. Listening to her heartbeat made him cry how slow, steady the rhythm were. He entered her. He felt the inhale and exhale of her breathing, continuing to listen to her heartbeat. Indulging in the warmth of being inside her. He didn't want to hurt her internally. He pressed harder each time. Allowing each one of her breathe to release her lungs, as he felt the hot air exhale from her lips. The vagina balls she had been using came in handy with the last press. She began to squeeze the tip of his penis. It made it so sensitive that he had an orgasm. It was like his body was having a grandma seizure. This happened for over ten minutes. The craziest thing was he was crying the whole time. It was a brother code to keep silent. I am glad that my brother was back. He wasn't the same guy after that. Peter had changed a little. We all still seeing if it was for the better. We will see eventually, but Chrissy knew the change was for good or bad. Ron still didn't miss a beat. Gracie had Ron balanced. We were seeing how she was so good for him. We were all started to move in living life. Nobody was behind anymore. We all were present.

Chapter Sixteen

It is year five of Chris death, we all decided to come to North Carolina for the summer to get together. Ron and Gracie were grandparents now. Peter and Chrissy created a non-profit for parents who lost a child in a tragic circumstance. Tina and I was praying together with churches and organizations believing to find Chris justice. That time with us on the beach was great. The guys met Mr. Tysmens. They enjoyed it because he told them stories of when I was growing up. He told the story of Ms. Pattello's ice cream shop. L.J. loves that story as well. I am grateful I didn't have to tell him the story. The guys and our wives went to the restaurant one evening for dinner. Our wives loved it! Tina knew how good it was because she can get it when she feels like it. These ladies don't get to taste this lovely food and the atmosphere that it brings. For some reason we didn't want to leave each other. We extended our trip that summer. We didn't know why we just knew it was for some reason only God knew. Everyone changed their schedules to stay at the beach an extra week. Mr. Tysmens was spoiled by our wives. They cooked him meals and freeze each of the meals, until they would spoil him again. He had meals to each for at least three months.

Chapter Seventeen

The guys all woke up that morning early. We walked out to the beach. We prayed together, sat and watched the sun rise over the ocean. We all talked how we could feel something in the air. We didn't know what, but had a feeling something was going to happen today. We thought our wives were still sleeping until we walked back to the house. Chrissy was cooking pancakes, Tina was cooking eggs and omelets, and Gracie was making fresh squeezed orange juice. We all greeted them and gave the smack on the butt in unison. The ladies all giggled. They knew what that meant. We were glad L.J. was staying at Mr. Tysmens. A lot of "12 play" was going on the grown folk's way. R. Kelly why, just why?

We went upstairs to take a quick wash up for breakfast. It was 9:15 a.m. on a Saturday morning. My cell phone ringed. It was the detective. I thought he was checking in to just let me know he had not given up on Chris case, etc. I sat down on the bed. Ron was in the bathroom and Peter was in the guest room. I answered the phone.

"Hello."

"Hello Leyton. This is Detective Hufftonington from the Prince William County, Virginia. I am calling because we have a break in the case."

"Great," I said. I was thinking something small or information about the girl.

"We found the girl's body in the Potomac River a month ago. We did not want to call you until we knew it was her, that we had the phone and some more information." Detective said.

"Okay, what is the news?" I asked.

"The young lady that Chris was helping was on drugs. He didn't know that she was connected to the mafia. Her name is Crystalynne Anne McMerri. She didn't tell him that. We learn that he knew her from back home. Chris was turning her around for the better. She grew up in a military home. When her father was killed in the Gulf War, she went down the wrong path. Chris was helping Crystalynne to get her life together. The divers found her phone. Chris and Crystalynne were falling in love. Chris was going to pay her way out. When the mafia found out that he was going to do that, they got upset. They had one of their hit men to kill Chris. Leyton your prayers had not gone in vain, sir."

I was sitting on the bed. It felt like I was sinking in the bed farther. Chris died for love, helping someone, and trying to give them a better life. I put the phone on speaker because I couldn't say a word. I couldn't even move. I was breathless. Peter heard the detective voice. He went to get Tina. She came upstairs, saw that I was motionless. She hugged me. I couldn't even cry. It was a relief that couldn't be explained.

"Lieutenant, Lieutenant! Are you there?" exclaimed the detective.

"Hello Detective. This is his wife Le Tina. You can call me Tina. Leyton can't speak right now. He is overwhelmed with the news."

"I apologize. Maybe I shouldn't give him so much at one time," he said.

"No. This was fine. Sometimes when God answers your prayers. It is more than you expected. "God do exceedingly abundantly above you could ask or think." (Ephesians 3:20, KJV), said Tina.

"Well, I do understand what that feeling is like. God is amazing. I will let you all digest this information for now. I will give you a call in a few more days with the information on the arrest," detective said.

"Yes, thank you. You have been faithful. I pray for God's blessing. Have you informed Chris' mother?" She asked.

"Yes, I told her to not to let Leyton know. I wanted to surprise him."

"Detective you have done just that!"

Tina hanged up the phone. Everyone came and gave me a group hug. I couldn't say nothing but cry for hours. When Chris' mother and Brody called me. I cried harder. I have to say I could believe in God more. My faith in God is stronger than ever. God told me to get the people of God to pray for a reason. God wanted to show me how powerful and how well he listens. Now it is my turn to learn how to listen.

Chapter Eighteen

I knew how to listen. I am learning how to listen to the hearts and not the words that people say. Their words don't match what their hearts are saying. Everyone stayed an extra three days. We wanted to celebrate and thank God for finding Chris justice. "Vengeance is mine; I will repay, saith the Lord" (Romans 12:20, KJV). I know that God's word is true. We all have been taught about God. It is up to us to have a relationship with God. When I think about how I carried the deaths of Charlesten and Carl, I couldn't believe how long I carried the deaths of those two soldiers. I blamed myself because I didn't know how to release that pain. I understand now it wasn't my fault. I guess when I love someone, I love so hard that I don't know if I should care sometimes. Do caring too much make me weak? I learn that this is how God made me. I have to accept that I have to protect what God has given me. It is too precious to give away to the dogs or pigs, like God said in His word. The ones who want to receive it. You give! You give it all! You don't know who you are changing for the better. He or she might not have a relationship with God like you. You will give them something that he or she can hold on too. The best things you can hold on too aren't visible but invisible. God is not dead, he is alive.

Chapter Nineteen

God has shown himself to me. I can't never forget this amazing moment of God's presence during that week. I knew I can't explain this feeling of knowing Chris death has received justice. Things don't happen when we want it but God will do it in his timing. I finally got that last phone call from Chris' mother. She was so excited, overwhelmed and praising God for doing this for her son. She had to remember that she taught him about God. She gave him God just like her parents did for her. She is grateful that she raised him in the fear and admiration before God. She believes her son is in heaven with God. If her son didn't have an open heart, she wouldn't have people in her life, like myself, Tina, Peter, Chrissy and Ron. She was grateful for Peter and Chrissy doing the foundation. She is now taken care of for life. Brody call her three to four times a week. Since Chris died, I can't imagine my life without all the people I love. I know how much my son was taken care of while he was away from home. When you said he was your son, God have shown that he was the son of all. Everybody protected him. When he said he was fine. I know he was fine.

"Leyton, thank you for trusting God. You had to listen to God to come up with getting the people to pray for his justice. I am glad you didn't go and search on your own. We could've lost you too."

It was those words that open my mind and heart to let me know, God was looking out for me. He wanted to see if I would communicate and trust him all the way. I see that now! I will trust God all the way. Detective Hufftonington believed in God as well, but he didn't believe like I did. Now, he takes his family to church. He spends more time with his family, especially his wife. His wife thanked you the first time we met. I told her it wasn't me. It was God. I was obedient when he said to pray for Chris justice. I didn't know that lives would be touched the way it was. I learned that God doesn't tell you to do something without a reason. I see this was the reason. He wanted people to see him. I realized that people didn't see God in the world anymore. The people getting together to pray was showing that God was still there. God wanted to be invited in our lives. He was a God of choice. He is a gentleman. I even learned to be more of a gentleman. One of the fruits of the spirits is gentle. Do we know how to be gentle with people and with our family?

This is a question that is for anyone who is trying to find, looking or even searching for an understanding of God. People aren't gentle with people anymore. I believe also this is why mental health is on the rise in the world. When I said this process has changed me, God allowed me to see things totally different. I don't see things in the way that others see the world. You don't have to travel the whole world to be wise. If you have God, then you have the world in the palm of your hand.

I feel like I am rambling. I hope I am making sense. We don't think what we are saying is important sometimes. What we have to say is important. We don't understand, but it is for someone. God let us know it is for someone. The question is who?

God knows the person. I just sit back and watch. I don't know who, why or how, but I do know the answer is God. I didn't understand when the older people would say God is the answer.

Yes! God is the answer! He is the answer to every situation. I can't stop saying that God showed me this in Chris' death.

Chapter Twenty

I went to a secluded location that I wanted to visit, but Tina did not want to go. It was by the water. It was more like a lake, I enjoyed fishing. This is where God spoke to me the most. I don't understand his one-word conversations at times. When it makes sense, all I can do is laugh. "A merry heart does good, like medicine" (Proverbs 17:22, NKJV). I enjoy to laugh. Most of all God sense of humor is so profound it shocks you. The more wisdom of God, the more is your life built beyond the foundation.

That time alone with God allowed me to heal more. God reveal some things I didn't understand before. God allow us to carry some things because we take the burden on ourselves. Are we in control? We as humans don't have any power. We have free will. Our heavenly father is a gentleman. He let us make the choices to receive our consequences. When we see that life don't have to be that way, that is when we look to a higher power or universe some people calls it. I know he is God. I can't say enough how in Chris' death, God showed himself strong, wise, powerful and all knowing. I had my cell phone, but didn't even open it. I just read the Bible, sat in silence, enjoyed my fishing and slept. I didn't really sleep in the military. I always had to be alert. You are sleeping but not asleep, because your mind isn't resting. Your mind is listening for sounds. That sound could be danger. This place I should have been on alert. Instead, God gave me a peace that was beyond my understanding. I left that early Saturday morning before 6:00 a.m. It was a five-hour drive. I took my time going back home. I stopped to enjoy the scenery. I took pictures of nature, which is the beauty of God creation. When I stopped for food or gas, I indulged in the conversations with the people I met. I had so much fun, that it felt I was living for the first time. I was! A five-hour drive was eight hours. I enjoyed the moment. I drove up in the driveway. Tina was going to the car. She stopped, turn and ran back in the house to tell L.J. They didn't allow me to get my stuff out of the car. I just soaked in the love from their hugs. It seemed like hours, but it was minutes. I took it all in. Once they were ready to release me. They helped me to get my bags out of the truck. Tina took my bags upstairs. When I got to the door, I smelled Tina's chicken and rice cooking in the crock pot. Tina isn't a Sunny Anderson in the kitchen. She can cook these simple meals that you think she slaved over a stove. When I found out her secret, I laughed. I had gone to be alone for a week. Tina and L.J. talked my ears off. Tina called Mr. Tysmens to ask if L.J. could stay for a few days.

Mr. Tysmens said, "Tina I was married before. Your husband was gone for a whole week and you cooked his favorite meal. I know."

After we ate dinner, L.J. and I talked some more, while Tina cleaned the kitchen. I offered to help. She whispered for me to save my energy. L.J. didn't want to leave me. I didn't want him either. I was ready for Tina. I remembered what Peter had told me. I called Peter while Tina was taking L.J. to Mr. Tysmens. Peter inform me that Tina had been talking to Chrissy. She has something planned for me. I let Peter know the experience I had with God while I was there. I wanted him and the guys to go and get a better relationship with God. Peter didn't say much, but he listened to what God had given me about husbands and men of their household. He agreed that he needed to do better. Peter rushed me off the phone, so I could get ready to spend time with Tina. I rushed upstairs to our guest bathroom to take a shower. I heard her come in the house. She ran upstairs to take a shower. I sat on the bed with the towel in my hands. She came out looking for the towel. I didn't say a word, but dried her off with the towel. I just smelt her. She smelled like that Dove Pink Rose. Inhaling the aroma of her, aroused me to the point that I wanted to make love to her right there. I calmed myself down. I sat on the bed. I wanted her to come sit between my legs. We sat in our nakedness, imperfections and silence. Tina got cold, I put the covers over her. Tina continued to snuggle against my chest. I believed that she listened to my heartbeat, but I felt her love. I know my wife loves me. I have been slacking in other ways to show her in return. Sex isn't the only way to show your wife love and intimacy. That night I showed her intimacy in a way that Tina was not used to. Tina woke up. She looks at me like she didn't know who I was.

"Who are you?" Tina asked. I chuckled. I gently kissed Tina. She touches my face, looking into my eyes, God allowed me to see into her soul. It scared me. I jumped back. I couldn't believe I saw that!

Tina thought she had touched me somewhere or hurt me. She didn't! I just had my first spiritual experience. I saw where she had a miscarriage while I was deployed. She never told me. I couldn't understand why it took her so long to get pregnant. I thought it was from her being sexually molested as a child. That wasn't it. She had some damage in one of her tubes. I pulled her close to hug her. I held her so tight, that I frightened her.

"L, you are scaring me. What is it?" She asked. I took a deep breath.

"Why you didn't tell me you had a miscarriage while I was deployed?" I asked.

Tina faced dropped. "How did you know?" She asked.

"God."

Tina burst in tears. The tears were running down her face like a fountain.

"I am not angry or upset Tina. I didn't understand why you didn't tell me." I sighed.

"L, you carried so much when you came home. Also, you experienced so much trauma that I didn't want to add to the pain you were already feeling. I carried you. When you got free at the party. I could breathe again, too."

I put my head against hers. We cried together. We sat in the bed naked in silence and releasing the pain. We could hear our stomachs growling. We did not want food. We wanted each other. The questions of what we had to bring to a close. We began to heal together. Silence is powerful. I get it now. I didn't understand that for a long time. You don't have to always speak your mind or even let others know. The scripture on being discreet has so much wisdom. Proverbs 14:8, "The wisdom of the prudent is to discern his way." Tina has made some moves of being discreet to be a supportive wife and mother. I didn't tell her this why she loved Chris so much. It was Chris who was with her during my deployment and the miscarriage. Chrissy didn't even know, Chris carried her during that hard time in her life. She would say she had doctor appointments or visiting one of the ladies in the neighborhood. Tina went to her therapist appointments. The miscarriage messed with her mind and emotions. I'm curious even the more what she is thinking or feeling. I just thought she was quiet because it was her new thing of wanting to be in silence. The silence was the pain of carrying that miscarriage. She will never know what our child look like, what it would be become, and carry him or her in her arms. It makes sense why Tina cries when she holds a newborn baby.

Still holding her in my arms healing in silence with our thoughts. I gently turned her face to me.

"Tina do you want to adopt a child?" I asked. Her eyes got so big. The tears begin to roll down her cheeks as a slow drizzle. She couldn't speak, just laid her head on my chest. I hope that means yes or needs to think about it. She gets up off the bed, walks around the room to get her bath robe to go downstairs. I guess that question deserved some food to think on.

All this time I was carrying the soldiers, really but that moment I was feeling Tina's pain of losing our child. "Chris you aren't here on this earth. Thank you for taking care of my wife." This is the reason she would fuss or get so upset when people would hurt or take your kindness for weakness. Chris was Tina's strength and support. He taught her the word of God to get through the hard time in her life. Smiling thinking about Chris, I hear Tina coming back upstairs. I heard her pause before she got inside the room. I thought maybe she needed to use the bathroom. I didn't hear the hall bathroom door open. I peaked in the hallway. I didn't see her. I yelled, "Tina! Tina!" I got off the bed to go look for her. She met me at the bedroom door. She had a Ziploc bag with a sandwich cut in half, a bottle of water and a bottle of my protein shakes. I took everything out of her arms and hands. I placed it on the night stand. When I turned around she had dropped her bath robe. I wasn't expecting that! The way the sun was reflecting through the closed blinds made Tina's skin have a glow. I took two shots of that protein shot. She chucked.

"I love this new Leyton. Will you make love to me?" She asked. I carried her to the bed. I placed her on the bed like it was an altar. The understanding that my wife is my first ministry. I know God has really changed me. I was asking God how to please my wife sexually. I thought it was inappropriate. God gave me Tina. I heard God say "paper". I took a piece of paper from the notepad on the night stand. I balled it up, then pulled it open. I balled up the paper again. I placed it on her stomach, representing where the baby that would've been in the womb. I laid between her legs as I was slowly blowing the ball of paper from her stomach up to her chest. The warmth of my breath and coolness of each blow was arousing my wife. I continued until she was laughing, giggling, arching her back, and grabbing the covers. As I continued to play with the paper over her body. Tina's laugh was bringing joy to my heart. I waited until I hear God to touch her with any part of my body. I couldn't kiss her. That piece of paper being blown up and down her body showed the freedom of being playful. The delicacy of a woman's body. I heard, "Now." I knew that I could enter my wife. When I entered, Tina had an organism. It poured from her like a faucet. I repositioned her by getting her close to the edge of the bed. If I attempt to go deeper into her, I would feel weak and nervous. When I figured out how to work with how far I could go. I studied her reactions, moans and grins.

People enter our world, but we only give how far he or she can go into our lives. When you have a mate, spouse, you can't just put them where you want them to be or how far to go. The other person is going to give their all, so will you? Can you give them your all with a limited number of space? When I studied her reactions, I found the spot. Tina turned red like she had rashes in certain areas of her body, toes bent, and pulling the covers from the bed. I felt wetness of my feet. The orgasm was so strong. Tina gave a holla that came from the pits of her belly. It poured as if her water broke again. Tina passed out. I played with her body while she was out. She woke up, pushed me on the bed and got on top of me.

"Stop teasing me, new Leyton." She said in a soft demanding voice. The way she had rode me was different. I felt the intensity of the climax building together. We both came at the same time. I remember before passing out, I was holding her so tight because what I was feeling so good that I put her breast in my mouth to not to scream like a girl. While I was out I had a dream of Chris standing in place that I couldn't tell where we were. He didn't say anything but just stood there laughed and smile. Then this little girl came from behind him. In my head, I was asking was this my child. Chris just nodded his head to say yes. Staring at the little girl, she looked like Tina and L.J. She was beautiful with her pigtails. She said, "Hi Daddy." Then she disappeared. Chris saluted me, then he was gone. This is what you called a sweet dream.

www.ingramcontent.com/pod-product-compliance
Lightning Source LLC
LaVergne TN
LVHW010606070526
838199LV00063BA/5093